WHERE I LIVE

FRANCES WOLFE

Tundra Books

Published in Canada by Tundra Books,
481 University Avenue, Toronto, Ontario M5G 2E9

Published in the United States by Tundra Books of Northern New York,
P.O. Box 1030, Plattsburgh, New York 12901

Library of Congress Control Number: 00-135459

National Library of Canada Cataloguing in Publication Data

Wolfe, Frances
Where I live

ISBN 0-88776-529-7

1. Seashore – Juvenile poetry.   I. Title.

PS8595.O588W43 2001   j793.73   C00-932286-8
PZ8.3.W64Wh 2001

We acknowledge the support of the Canada Council for the Arts and the
Ontario Arts Council for our publishing program.

We acknowledge the financial support of the Government of Canada
through the Book Publishing Industry Development Program
for our publishing activities.

Design: Kong Njo

Medium: oil on Masonite

Printed in Hong Kong, China

2 3 4 5 6   06 05 04 03 02 01

For Mom and Dad, who provided the safe joyful

place from which I have drawn the inspiration

for the quiet childhood memories found in this book.

Sunbeams

sparkle

like

diamonds

on water

and

gulls glide

on morning

breezes,

where I live.

Engines

push great

ships

through

water

and

oars pull

my small boat

over the waves,

where I live.

A fternoons

we spend

picking

wild

blueberries

and

finding

figures hidden

in the clouds,

where I live.

S pecial

treasures are

found on

sun-warmed

sands

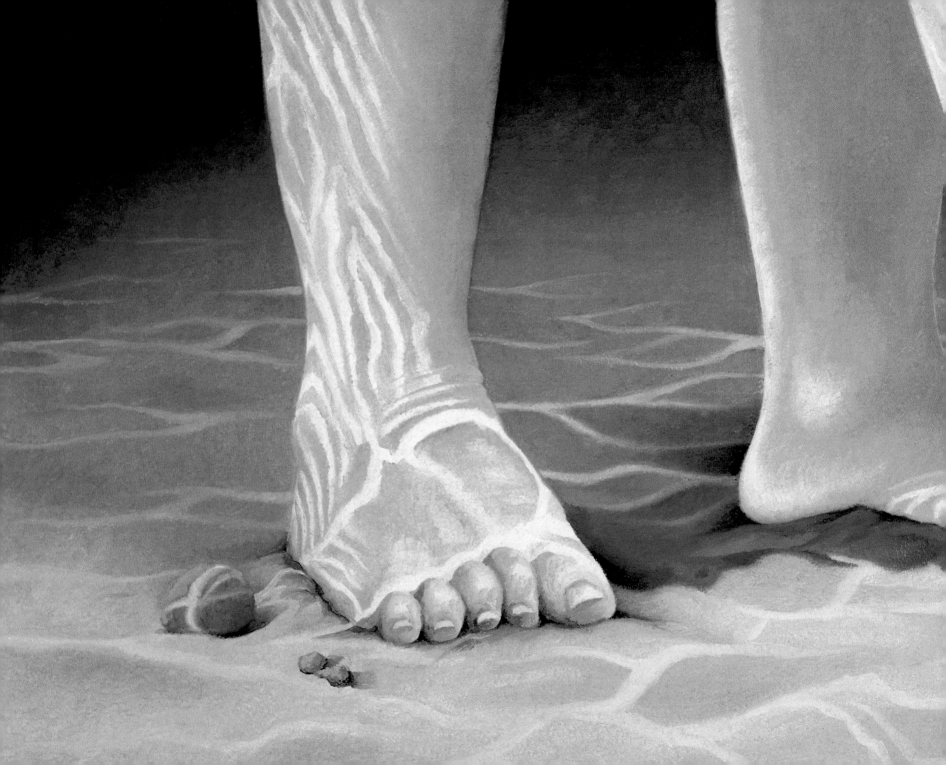

and

in the

cool green

waters,

where I live.

Images

appear

in the

flickering

firelight

and

lamplight

leads ships to

safe harbors,

where I live.

D reary

days

bring

drops

of rain

and

I read

stories to

pass the time,

where I live.

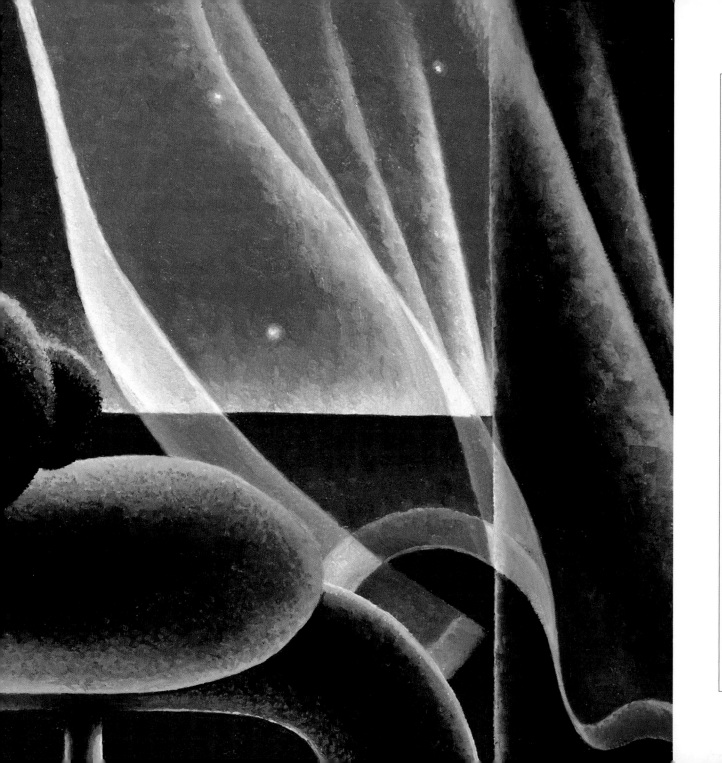

E vening

breezes

dance with

my bedroom

curtains

and

bring sweet

dreams and

tender sleep,

where I live.

Where I live . . . the S E A S I D E.

and

bring sweet

dreams and

tender sleep,

where I live.

Where I live . . . the S E A S I D E.